THE BOOK OF
AURORA

THE BOOK OF AURORA

A Woman at the Threshold

Lady Glamourgan

The Book of Aurora
A Woman at the Threshold

Published by House of Glamourgan™
House of Glamourgan, LLC
Olympia, Washington, USA

First edition, February 2026
www.houseofglamourgan.com
www.glamourgan.uk
ISBN: 979-8-9948156-0-1
Printed in the United States of America

Cover, interior design and formatting by:
www.emtippettsbookdesigns.com

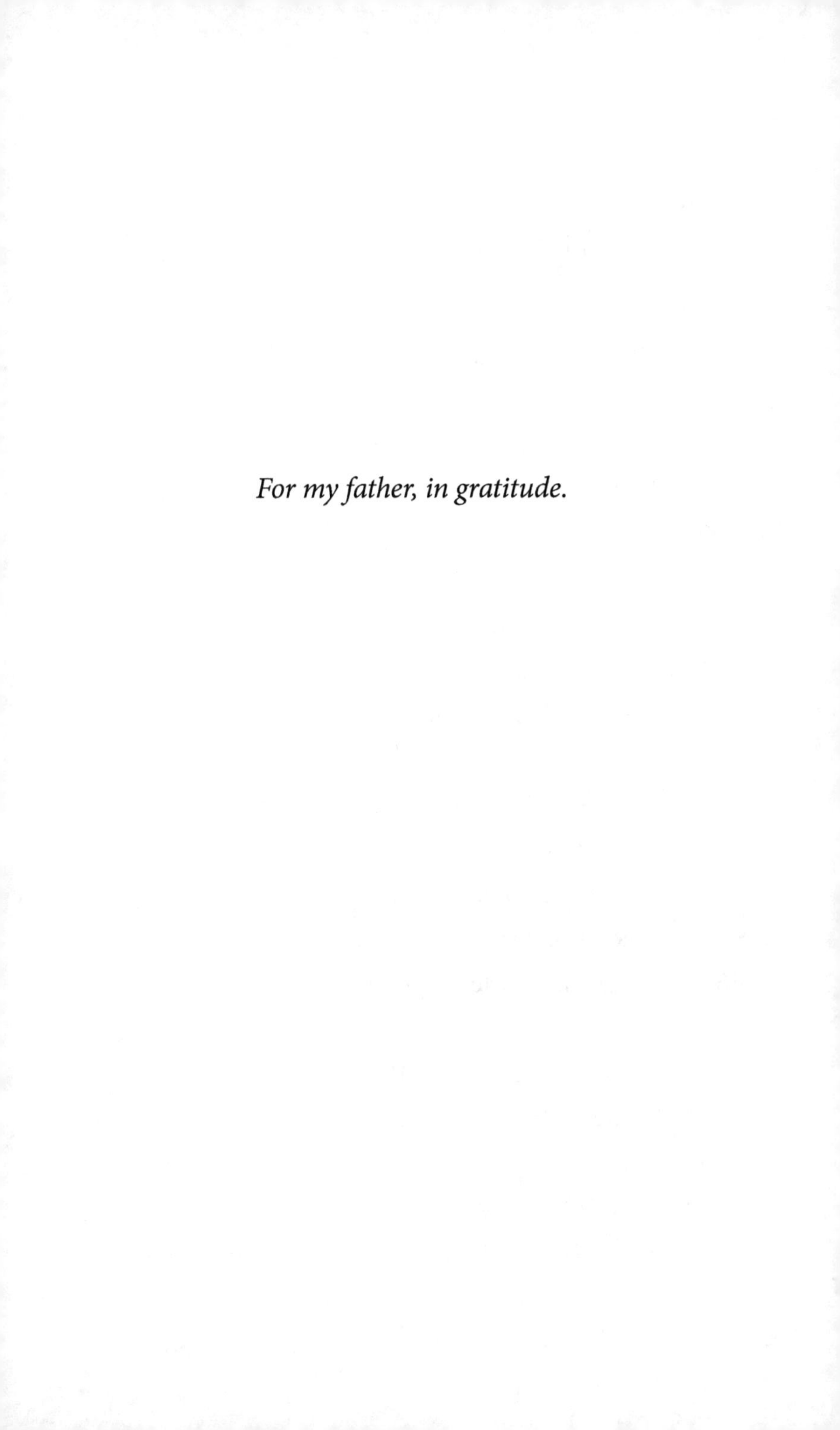

For my father, in gratitude.

TABLE OF CONTENTS

PROLOGUE

The Night Something Inside Her Finally Broke

Aurora did not know this would be the night that split her life into before and after.

She didn't know that the woman she had been for decades was about to dissolve like mist under sunlight.

She only knew this:

Something inside her had cracked.

A clean, inner fissure — quiet but undeniable.

The kind that appears the moment you can no longer pretend.

It happened long after midnight.

The world outside her window was still, washed in a soft halo of blue from the lone streetlamp on the corner.

Its light fell in a thin, trembling line across her bedroom floor — the only witness to her unraveling.

Her phone lay on the bed beside her, screen dark, cold as a stone.

Hours earlier, she'd sent a simple message:

"Are you still awake?"

She knew he wasn't.

She knew he shouldn't be.

She knew exactly where he was —

and exactly where she wasn't.

And yet, she waited.

Because she always waited.

Aurora waited for men who forgot her.

For promises that evaporated.

For clarity that never came.

For love that demanded her patience, her power, her nights, her longing —

while giving little in return.

Tonight the weight of all her waiting settled on her chest like a stone.

The blue light from the lamp flickered outside — just once — as though the universe blinked with her.

She rose from the bed slowly, drawn toward the cool spill of light across the room.

Her shadow stretched long behind her, as if the past version of her were still clinging, refusing to let go.

She looked at her reflection in the soft blue glow.

Not broken.

Not angry.

Not defeated.

Just… done.

Done with the silence.

Done with the ambiguity.

Done with negotiating for crumbs.

Done with mistaking chaos for connection.

Her breath caught — the kind you take when truth enters the body before the mind can protest.

Inside her, that thin crack widened.

And a whisper rose — steady, ancient, absolute:

“No-more.”

She didn’t say it to him.

She didn’t say it to the past.

She didn’t say it out of rage or grief.

She said it to herself.

Because tonight wasn't about losing anyone.

Tonight was about reclaiming the woman she had misplaced inside a thousand soft excuses.

She touched her heart, felt its tired rhythm, and realized:

She had been starving for a long time.

Not for affection.

Not for attention.

For alignment.

And once a woman realizes she is starving, she stops pretending the crumbs are enough.

The streetlamp outside hummed faintly — the sound of a world preparing to shift.

The crack inside her became a doorway.

The ache became a compass.

The darkness became a womb.

She stood there, bathed in the thin blue glow, and understood:

This is the last night I will ever abandon myself.

And somewhere in the distance — beyond heartbreak, beyond habit, beyond the life she was shedding —
the first shimmer of dawn began to rise.

Welcome to

THE BOOK OF AURORA

A Woman at the Threshold

PART I

The Unraveling

ONE

The Morning After

Morning comes as a thin, uncertain thing — a pale wash of light that doesn't quite warm the room. Aurora wakes slowly, as if surfacing from deep water.

The first thing she notices is the phone on the floor beside her bed, facedown, as if even it was exhausted by last night's unraveling. She doesn't pick it up. Not yet. The silence around it feels safer than whatever waits inside.

She pulls a wool wrap around her shoulders before standing. The air is colder than she expects — sharper, almost glacial — the kind of cold that makes the edges of the world feel too defined. She steps carefully, making her way across the room as though she must reintroduce herself to the act of moving.

When she passes the window, she glances out on instinct.

There, in the early hush, the distant streetlamp still glows blue — not touching the walls inside, but hovering outside like a lone sentinel. It is the last witness to who she was a few hours ago.

In the kitchen, the cold wood floor presses against her bare feet. Tile countertops hold the night's chill, as if the room has been holding its breath. She heats milk for hot chocolate, not because she's hungry — she isn't — but because the ritual of warmth feels like something her hands can hold onto. Something simple. Something hers.

She sits at the table and wraps both palms around the mug. The warmth doesn't quite reach her chest yet. Everything feels… slightly farther away than it should. The chair beneath her. The texture of the wool. The weight of her own breathing.

Not numb. Not detached.

Just… quiet inside.

As if her body hasn't caught up to the truth her spirit already absorbed last night.

She doesn't replay what happened.

She doesn't think of him — not directly, not in the way she used to.

What rises instead is the stranger sensation of space.

A widening.

A gentle, unfamiliar question hovering at the edge of her awareness:

If not this… then what?

She stares into the steam curling above the mug, noticing how it dissolves into the air. She feels, with startling clarity, that the world around her is still intact — the floor, the light, the mug — but she is not the same woman who stood in that blue glow the night before.

There is a hollow ache where a tether used to be.

There is also the faintest pulse of possibility beneath it.

For the first time in a long time, she wonders — not about him, not about what he will do next — but about herself.

About the life she wants.

About the woman she could become.

About the quiet promise she made to her own soul the moment something inside her finally cracked open:

I don't have to live like this anymore.

I deserve better than this.

A sudden brightness pulls her attention —
the lamp outside flickers and goes dark
just as the first rays of sunlight slice through the window, sharp and blinding.

She stands, moves into the hallway, and turns the thermostat up to seventy.

The soft hum begins almost instantly.

Back in her bedroom, she slips on thick wool socks and crawls beneath her down blanket, the wrap still gathered around her shoulders. The warmth begins to settle around her in slow, deliberate waves.

She sinks deeper into the blanket, breathing slowly.
The room is beginning to warm.
So is something inside her — subtle, steady, unmistakable.
She doesn't rush to define it.
She simply sits with it, letting the morning gather around her.
There is a quiet she hasn't felt in years.
Not the quiet of absence.
The quiet of recognition.
The moment a woman stops negotiating with her own spirit…
and starts listening.

And in that stillness —
the deeper truth begins to rise.

Aurora stays beneath the blanket for a moment, letting the quiet gather around her.

The quiet settles differently now — less like emptiness, more like a space she didn't know she needed.

Women imagine that these turning points come as thunder.

But they arrive like this —

a single morning where the truth is finally louder than the habit.

A hundred small dismissals.

A thousand moments of waiting.

A lifetime of rearranging herself so someone else could stay comfortable.

All of it builds, grain by grain, until a woman finally hears the one voice she has ignored the longest:

Her own.

It comes without drama — soft, steady, unmistakably hers.

She doesn't stop caring about him.

She doesn't shut her heart.

But something shifts in its direction, almost imperceptibly.

The question is no longer "Does he want me?"
It becomes "Why did I abandon myself for so long?"
And then another truth unfolds quietly behind it —
one she didn't realize until now:
She made him the center of her world.
And now she wants to place herself back at the center of her own life.
It doesn't feel selfish.
It feels sane.
Because when a woman stops asking what she did wrong, she finally sees what was real.

Aurora sinks deeper into the warmth of the blanket. She feels present in a way she hasn't in months —
not healed, but returned to herself.

A slow breath leaves her, calm, grounded, certain.

This is the beginning of understanding why strong women bond with the Unlit Masculine:

men whose inner fire has never fully ignited,
men unfinished in themselves,
men who cannot hold what they reach for —
not because they don't feel,
but because they are not yet lit from within.

And Aurora knows now:

She will not walk toward that kind of unlit flame again.

The First Knowing

There is a kind of knowing that does not announce itself.

It does not arrive as certainty or courage or plans.

It arrives as stillness.

As the absence of striving.

As the body loosening its grip on a story it has carried for too long.

Aurora does not call it awakening yet.

She only knows that something inside her has gone quiet in a way that feels honest.

The pattern is still ahead of her.

The understanding is still forming.

The threshold has not yet appeared.

But the first door has closed.

And in the soft dark of this ordinary night,

her life has already begun to turn

TWO
The Chaos Pattern

Why Strong Women Bond with the Unlit Masculine

Aurora had always believed her heartbreaks were isolated events — different men, different circumstances, different lives she tried to build from thin threads of almost-connection.

But patterns form long before a woman recognizes them. They take shape quietly, forming the architecture under her choices, her longing, her blind spots, her hope.

The chaos pattern began long before the first text message that made her chest tighten. It began in the earliest version of Aurora — the part of her that learned to interpret inconsistency as depth, and uncertainty as desire.

Women who grow up navigating emotional weather — whether from parents, early partners, or the world around them — develop a sensitivity that feels like intuition but is often hypervigilance in a softer disguise. They learn how to read a room before they read themselves. How to soothe others before they soothe their own wounds. How to anticipate withdrawal, distance, silence — and confuse that anticipation with connection.

The Unlit Masculine does not consciously seek out this kind of woman. His unfinished heart simply gravitates toward someone who can metabolize his inconsistency without collapsing. And she, in turn, confuses his unpredictability with passion.

Not because she is naïve.

But because her nervous system was once trained to expect instability — and to call it love.

The chaos pattern is born exactly there: in the subconscious recognition of familiarity.

Familiarity — The Perfect Storm.

The body remembers old storms even when the mind has forgotten.

Something in her recognizes that this is not just a moment, but part of a longer pattern — a story her body has been living for years.

The Familiarity Trap

Aurora once sat across from a man who spoke in soft tones about growth, healing, awakening. He looked at her as though she was a revelation he hadn't been prepared to meet. She believed him. Why wouldn't she? His eyes warmed when he spoke. His voice softened.

And yet — something in her tightened every time he pulled away.

That tension felt like chemistry.

But it wasn't attraction.

It was anticipation.

Anticipation becomes activation.
Activation becomes attachment.
Attachment becomes longing.
Longing becomes self-betrayal.

This is the sequence women rarely name. Aurora lived it more times than she admitted, even to herself.

The Unlit Masculine does not intend to create this cycle. He simply does not know how to stop disappearing into himself. He offers surges of connection — flashes of tenderness that feel like prophecy — followed by emotional stillness that feels like abandonment.

A woman in her depth will always try to bridge the gap. She thinks patience is the medicine.

But here is the truth:

What she thinks is chemistry is actually her nervous system trying to resolve an old wound through a new man.

And the chaos pattern feeds on unresolved history.

The Invisible Contract

Every chaotic relationship begins with an invisible agreement — the kind a woman does not consciously make.

He will offer flashes of tenderness, and she will translate them into promises.

He will drift into silence, and she will fill it with meaning.

He will withdraw, and she will lean in — because the pattern has trained her to perceive distance as an invitation.

This contract is never spoken aloud.

It is felt.

It is remembered in the body, activated by the faintest trace of inconsistency.

And yet, despite its silence, she signs it every time with her hope. Because she learned long ago that if she could be patient enough, soft enough, empathic enough, intuitive enough, she could earn the emotional safety she was never freely given.

The Masculine Who Never Learned to Stay Anchored

He does not know he is participating in this contract.

He is not malicious — just unlit.

A man who never learned to sit with his own fear cannot stay present with someone who feels deeply. Her emotional fluency overwhelms him; her presence unsettles him; her insight threatens to expose the rooms inside himself he keeps locked.

So he does what unlit men do: he offers connection in pulses — a moment of warm intensity, a conversation that feels like revelation, a touch that makes her believe he has finally arrived.

And then — absence.

Not rejection.

Not negation.

Just disappearance into the uncharted territory of his own inner world.

He does not know how to hold what he awakens, or how to match the depth he evokes, or how to metabolize intimacy without retreat. His light flickers because he never learned how to tend it.

Aurora's First Flicker of Recognition

Something in her knows this rhythm.

Knows it too well.

A quiet awareness stirs beneath her ribs — a whisper, not yet a truth:

This feels familiar.

But familiarity is seductive. It masquerades as destiny. It tells her the tightening in her chest is a sign, not a warning.

Still — this time, something is different.

Her body responds before her mind does. A small, almost imperceptible shift: instead of leaning toward him, she leans toward herself.

It is barely a movement — more like a breath turning — but it is the beginning.

Aurora is studying her-story — herstory.

The Perfect Storm is no longer unconscious.

The architecture of the chaos pattern is beginning to take shape in her awareness.

She doesn't resist it yet.

She doesn't escape it yet.

She doesn't break it yet.

But she sees it.

And sight is the first crack in any spell.

The Cost of the Contract

She does not notice the cost at first. No woman ever does. The contract begins with small forfeitures — the kind that masquerade as compromise.

Her voice softens. Not because she lacks conviction, but because she senses his fragility and adjusts herself into something consumable.

Her boundaries thin. Not because she is weak, but because she has learned that asserting herself results in distance — and distance feels like danger to a nervous system shaped by inconsistency.

Her intuition dims. Not because it is faulty, but because she has spent years overriding its warnings in exchange for emotional crumbs labeled as love.

She abandons herself in increments too subtle to name —

a swallowed truth,
a postponed need,
a silenced instinct,
a heart held slightly off to the side.

By the time the cost becomes visible, she is already deep inside the architecture of the pattern. The dimming happened long before the heartbreak. The heartbreak is simply the evidence.

The Seduction of Potential

This is where the pattern casts its most beautiful illusion. The Unlit Masculine never shines steadily, but when he flickers, oh — it is luminous.

His warmth arrives in flashes — a tender moment here, a vulnerable admission there, a rare confession that makes her believe she is the one he will finally choose to grow for.

She bonds not to the man before her, but to the man he could be — the man he might discover within himself if only he loved her enough, if only life softened him, if only he healed.

The fantasy becomes its own gravitational pull.

A single good day erases a week of distance.

A heartfelt message compensates for a month of silence.

A moment of passion convinces her that the story is building toward a turning point he is secretly preparing.

Almost becomes intoxicating.

Almost becomes hope.

Almost becomes the tether.

It is not delusion. It is the ancient survival strategy of women raised on the promise that if they are loving enough, patient enough, forgiving enough, they will earn what should have been given freely.

Potential becomes the altar where she lays her longing down.

The Breaking of the Spell (Part One)

The first fracture never arrives as a shout. It arrives as a whisper.

A moment — barely a moment — when his absence feels heavier than his presence. When she says something true and he slips sideways rather than meeting her eyes.

When his story contradicts itself and her intuition flickers like lightning behind the clouds.

A question forms, quiet but undeniable:

Is this love… or self-erasure?

It is the first honest question she has asked in the relationship. Not the kind that seeks reassurance. Not the kind that asks who he is. But the kind that asks who she is becoming in the presence of his inconsistency.

And in that moment — a moment he may never even notice — the spell loosens.

Her awareness rises like distant thunder — a sound she feels in her bones before she hears it in her ears.

This is not the awakening. That comes later, when she stands at the threshold of a much greater truth.

This is the pre-awakening — the crack in the lens, the first lightning strike in a sky that has been gathering for years.

Aurora doesn't leave. Not yet. But something in her stops bending. Some part of her refuses to go dim again.

And once a woman feels that refusal — even faintly — the pattern no longer has her in the same way.

The unraveling has begun.

The Quiet Before the Knowing

There is a moment in every woman's transformation that cannot be named — a place between seeing the pattern and being ready to step beyond it.

It is not clarity, not yet, but it is no longer confusion either. It is the quiet middle ground where awareness has taken root but action has not yet unfolded.

Aurora stands there now.

She says nothing about it. Strong women rarely confess the moment they begin to awaken. They do not announce their unraveling or their becoming. They simply start listening differently — not to him, but to themselves.

Her inner world, long muted by caretaking and endurance, begins to hum with a new frequency. A soft truth rises beneath her thoughts:

Something is happening in me.

Not because he changed.

Because she did.

This is the phase of subtle rebellion — when a woman's silence is no longer compliance but contemplation, when a faint question lingers behind every breath, when she begins to gather pieces of herself she did not realize she had set aside.

Awareness is a slow unfurling. It moves like water through stone — persistent, unhurried, undeniable.

Aurora is not ready to leave the chaos pattern, but she is no longer completely inside it either. She stands at the threshold between who she has been and who she is becoming — a woman who knows, who sees, who remembers her own light.

And once a woman remembers — even faintly — the world she accepted begins to feel too small.

Chapter Three begins the moment she stops trying to make herself fit.

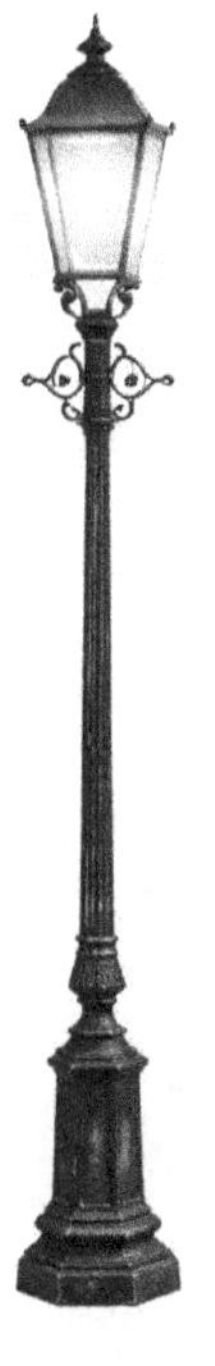

PART II

The Threshold

THREE

Threshold

Aurora wakes with the sense that she is standing inside a liminal space — the quiet, sacred region between who she has been and who she is becoming. The morning carries a different weight today, a deeper clarity gathering within her soul. She feels a threshold rising inside her, a doorway into a life shaped by truth rather than endurance. The room mirrors yesterday, yet something within her moves with new awareness, as if the world has shifted half an inch toward possibility.

Thresholds appear when a woman's awareness reaches new depth.

They arrive when her thinking expands into wider horizons,
when her being shifts toward clarity,
when her spirit feels the opening into a future shaped by truth.

Aurora stands within this widening, sensing the moment when suffering releases its hold on her path. A gentler future presses toward her awareness, and her whole being leans in its direction. Through understanding, she feels the past loosening its architecture, and her awareness expands into a life that grows wider than the frame she once accepted.

This is the moment her truth gathers power.
The inner turning.
The quiet crossing into a new way of living.

She rests inside the threshold's light, present and alert, allowing her spirit to align with what comes next. This liminal space feels steady, luminous, unafraid — the beginning of a life that rises from clarity rather than pain.

Aurora breathes into this newness —
the space where her future begins to shape itself.

The Breaking of the Spell — (Part Two)

The morning air feels different today — clearer, quieter, as though something unseen has shifted around her.

Awareness moves differently once it takes root.

It begins quietly, almost imperceptibly, shaping her choices in ways she doesn't fully recognize at first.

Aurora moves through her day with a new kind of attention —

subtle, steady, observant.

Conversations feel thinner.

Silences feel sharper.

The places where she once bent instinctively now rise like small hills, asking her to step over rather than collapse into them.

She feels her spirit watching her life from a slightly higher vantage point, as though truth has lifted her onto a ledge where she can finally see the pattern with clarity rather than longing.

The old reflexes still flicker — reaching, softening, interpreting, hoping —

but they arrive with less persuasion now.

They feel like echoes of a previous version of herself rather than commands she must obey.

The spell begins to loosen through recognition.

Recognition reshapes the story.

The story reshapes her responses.

Aurora notices the small places where she once disappeared —

a paused breath,

a swallowed instinct,

a sudden drop of energy when his inconsistency brushed against her tenderness.

She sees these moments with new eyes, not with judgment but with understanding, as though her inner world is holding a lantern to the shadows she once navigated blindly.

She feels the shift most clearly in her body —

in the way her chest stays open during pauses,

in the way her breath remains steady during uncertainty,

in the way her shoulders no longer curl inward when she senses distance.

Her body understands the truth before her mind articulates it:

The pattern has lost its power over her.

Not through force.

Through seeing.

The spell breaks when the woman returns to herself.

The spell breaks when her awareness stays present.

The spell breaks the moment she realizes her worth is no longer tethered to someone else's capacity to meet her.

Aurora feels this realization rising through her like a quiet dawn.

She is not leaving anything yet.

She is not stepping forward or away.

She simply stands in her own presence with a steadiness she has not felt in years.

The universe shifts for a woman the moment she remembers her value.

Aurora feels that shift now —

a soft, unwavering pulse within her soul,

a reminder that she is moving toward a life where her light is fully met.

And in that inner turning,

the rest of the spell begins to fall away.

The Energetic Reversal

There is a moment in every unraveling where the energy shifts before the relationship does.

Aurora begins to feel it now — a subtle turning of the tide.

The part of her that once reached toward him without hesitation begins to grow still.

It is not resistance.

It is not punishment.

It is a return.

Her energy no longer pours outward by reflex.

It settles back into her, warm and steady, like water finding its own level.

And without her realizing it, something in him reacts.

Unlit men feel the shift before they understand it.

They sense when a woman's spirit is no longer orbiting their inconsistency.

They feel the field of attention change —

the pull lightens,

the center of gravity returns to her.

He cannot name it.

But he feels the difference in the silence between them.

Where she once bent, she now breathes.

Where she once filled the gap, she now observes it.

Where she once feared distance, she now recognizes it as information.

The reversal doesn't require confrontation.

It doesn't require a declaration.

It doesn't even require a change in behavior.

It is an inner shift —

a woman stepping back into herself,

and a man feeling the absence of the pedestal he never deserved.

And for the first time, she sees him clearly.

Not as the man she hoped he would become.

Not as the man she tried to interpret.

But as the man he has always been.

This is the beginning of emotional detachment —

the quiet, holy kind

that rises when truth finally outgrows illusion.

The Return to Herself

Aurora feels the shift before she names it — a quiet settling inside her, a slow reclaiming of the space she once surrendered without question. Her awareness gathers around her like a soft mantle, familiar and new at the same time, as though her soul has begun calling her back into the center of her own life.

Her energy moves differently now. It rises instead of reaching. It anchors instead of chasing. It returns instead of pouring outward.

She feels it first in her breath — deeper, steadier, no longer shaped around someone else's uncertainty. Then in her posture — her shoulders soften without collapsing, her spine lengthens without effort, her heart remains open without offering itself away.

A woman knows when she is coming back to herself. It feels like warmth returning to forgotten places.

She notices the small things first — how her thoughts no longer orbit his attention, how her emotions no longer hinge on his presence, how her spirit no longer contracts to make room for his contradictions.

The inner landscape shifts quietly, but unmistakably.

Where she once scanned for signs from him, she now listens for signals from within. Where she once shaped herself to create harmony, she now allows truth to stand as it is. Where she once feared losing him, she now recognizes the cost of losing herself.

The return is not dramatic. It is intimate. Holy. Deeply private.

A woman does not announce the moment she stops abandoning herself. She simply begins to inhabit her own life again.

Aurora feels this awakening as a subtle fullness — a sense of being home in her own body, her own wants, her own clarity.

This is the true turning point. Not the end of the pattern. The end of her participation in it.

She rises into herself gently, and in that rising everything begins to realign.

The Quiet Pivot

Aurora sits in the stillness of her own awareness, letting the truth settle without rushing to define it. There is no urgency, no declaration forming, no decision demanding movement. What rises within her is quieter than that — a shift in the center of her being, subtle but unmistakable. She feels as though she has stepped into a room inside herself that she had forgotten existed, a place where her worth is not questioned and her clarity is not dimmed.

She notices how steady she feels, how spacious her inner world becomes when she stops orienting every thought around his next move. The air inside her life feels different — clearer, calmer, less entangled. It is not resolve in the traditional sense. It is resonance. Alignment. The soft confirmation that she is returning to herself, one breath at a time.

This is the moment where the story pauses.

Not at an ending.

Not at a beginning.

At the quiet pivot between them.

Aurora senses that the external world has not shifted yet, but her inner world has already chosen a different path. She is not preparing to leave. She is preparing to see. And in that seeing, everything she once tolerated begins to feel foreign to her spirit.

She rests here for a moment, allowing the insight to settle into her bones — the understanding that the pattern cannot continue when she no longer participates. Something inside her has crossed a threshold, and once crossed, she cannot unknow it.

And in the stillness of this interlude, Aurora understands:

the spell is not fully broken yet,
but she is no longer under it.

FOUR

The Path of Embodiment

The moment arrives gently — a shift in the inner horizon. Aurora wakes with a deeper awareness humming through her, a sense that her spirit is no longer trailing behind her life but rising to meet it. Her true center is illuminating — steady, radiant, and flowing — as though her soul has opened like a living river finding its natural course again.

Like the Maidenhair fern, a subtle widening unfurls inside her.

Her inner landscape expands in quiet revelation, and she feels the first warmth of embodiment rising through her.

She moves through her morning differently.

The air feels clearer.

Her steps feel grounded.

Her breath feels aligned with something ancient and trustworthy within her.

A woman recognizes this shift as a return —

a homecoming to the self she set aside

while tending to a love that could not hold her.

Awareness becomes orientation.

Orientation becomes embodiment.

Embodiment becomes the new way she walks through the world.

> This is the moment when her attention turns inward into her own path of restoration.

She explores.

She expands.

She inhabits.

> Her focus no longer circles him or the space between them.
>
> Her focus roots into her body, her breath, her presence.

She feels herself becoming her own home.

> The world meets her differently when she stands in this place.

People respond to the radiance she had forgotten was hers.

Experiences shift in subtle ways —

it is magnetic,

it is attraction,

because she is now encountering the world from her center rather than from depletion.

She feels possibility again,

she experiences freedom

and spaciousness.

This is the beginning of the real transformation —

the turning inward that reorients the whole of her life.

She is no longer navigating from longing or loss.

She is navigating from self-rooted clarity.

Her soul is speaking in a new language —

one of sovereignty, presence, and sacred remembering.

Embodiment is the path.

And Aurora is finally walking it.

The Body Remembers the Way Home

Aurora begins to notice something she hasn't felt in years — her body speaking first. Her mind may analyze, interpret, and negotiate, but her body tells the truth without hesitation. And that truth is rising. There is a groundedness in her hips, a soft warmth across her chest, a steadier rhythm in her breath that feels like a language she once knew by heart.

Her body becomes an altar of remembering — a place where intuition is not a puzzle but a path. She feels the shift when she walks across a room; her steps land differently now, with presence rather than seeking. She notices it in conversations too, when her attention remains rooted in her own energy instead of scanning the emotional weather of someone else.

But she feels it most powerfully in silence.

Silence used to collapse her.

Now it nourishes her.

This is the intelligence of embodiment —

the body holding ancient instructions for a woman's becoming,

guiding her back to herself long before her thoughts can name the direction.

Aurora feels this guidance rising like a steady pulse beneath her awareness. She follows it gently, instinctively —away from old patterns and into the deeper current inside her.

Every small act of noticing becomes a reclamation.

Every breath becomes an answer.

Every moment of presence becomes a doorway.

She is beginning to understand that embodiment is not a performance.

It is a relationship —

between her essence, her awareness, and the life returning within her.

Her body remembers the way home.

And for the first time in a long time,
Aurora is listening.

When Life Responds to a Woman in Her Center

Life begins to shift around Aurora the way the air changes when a storm clears — quietly, undeniably, with a sense of space returning to the horizon. People meet her eyes differently. Conversations land with more truth. The world registers her presence with a subtle reverence she hasn't felt in years.

This is what happens when a woman stands in her center.

Her energy reorganizes the field around her.

She moves through the day with an inner gravity

that does not pull her downward but draws life toward her — opportunities, clarity, synchronicities that seem to appear from nowhere. She notices that her intuition responds more quickly now, not as a warning system, but as a companion guiding her toward what is aligned.

Her voice feels clearer.

Her boundaries feel organic.

Her presence feels expansive.

The world responds to the shift inside her as though recognizing her true frequency — the one she abandoned when she dimmed herself for love that did not yet know how to meet her.

People speak to her differently.

Some soften.

Some reveal truths they held back before.

Some step closer, sensing the radiance returning to her field.

Aurora feels it all without absorbing any of it.

She stands in herself now — luminous, grounded, sovereign.

Her life begins to open in small but powerful ways:

A moment of unexpected kindness from a stranger.

A decision that feels effortless.

A conversation that lands with clarity instead of confusion.

A desire that rises without shame or hesitation.

A truth that feels like home when she says it out loud.

She realizes that this is the nature of embodied awakening —

the outer world rearranging itself to reflect the woman she has become.

Aurora is not waiting to be chosen anymore.

She is choosing her life.

And the moment she does,

life responds with precision,

meeting her at the level of her newfound clarity.

The path ahead does not unfold in one grand revelation.

It opens step by step, breath by breath,

in the subtle glow of her returning light.

She walks through her day with the sense that something vast within her is aligning —

a rhythm, a resonance, a destiny that had been waiting for her to rise.

Aurora is no longer shaped by what once held her.

She is shaping the world around her with the full presence of who she is becoming.

And the world — finally — responds in kind.

PART III

Sovereignty In Practice

FIVE

Discernment

What She Carries Forward

Aurora experiences discernment as an opening — a widening of her inner field that allows more of the world to come into view. Her thoughts move differently now, unhurried and spacious, as though her attention has learned how to rest inside herself.

She feels this most clearly in places she knows well.

The old bookshop has always been her special place — a place she visits often, a place that feels like home. She enters easily, the quiet welcome of it settling around her. The fresh scent of paper and ink, the soft hush of voices, the steady presence of shelves she has passed countless times before — all of it feels grounding, intimate, known. A world that speaks her language.

She turns first toward the café tucked inside the shop.

The barista looks up and smiles in recognition. They exchange a few easy words, a warmth that feels natural and unforced. Aurora notices the shift in herself gently: she feels present, open, at ease. The barista seems to notice it too — she smiles, a brightness, a lightness that hadn't been there for a long time has returned.

She orders her favorite comforting drink — hot chocolate, rich and warm — and wraps her hands around the mug as it's passed to her. The warmth settles into her palms, steadying her. It feels chosen, familiar, reassuring in a way that supports her rather than anchors her.

With her drink in hand, she begins to wander among the shelves.

This is where the change becomes unmistakable.

She has walked these aisles many times before, yet now her awareness opens in a new way. Sections that once sat quietly at the edges of her vision begin to draw her attention. Her eyes linger on colors, textures, and titles.

Philosophy.

Myth.

Women's history.

Art.

Cosmology.

The living world.

Stories that speak of sovereignty, imagination, depth.

A fresh current of curiosity moves through her — calm, alive, inviting.

She notices how fully she is here.

Before, her attention had been occupied elsewhere, quietly pulled inward by a single thread that shaped how she experienced every room. Now, her awareness belongs to the space itself. The shelves are rich with possibility. The tables hold quiet concentration. The room breathes with presence.

There are no associations tugging at her attention anymore.

The space meets her as it is.

What fills her awareness instead is the richness of the world.

She notices the way light falls across the spines of books. The gentle rhythm of the café — cups lifted, pages turned, people lingering without hurry. A woman a few tables away is absorbed in her reading, wholly present. All of it feels vivid, textured, alive.

She realizes that this world was always here.

Her vision has expanded.

Aurora understands something fundamental in this moment: she can live fully in the places she loves. She can remain rooted in her town, her rhythms, her familiar spaces — and experience freedom within them. Her life does not need to be replaced. It is revealing itself more completely.

She stops at a shelf and reaches for a book.

As she holds it in her hands, a quiet recognition settles into her body. This is the one. The book feels like a match. It strengthens something already present in her. Its story speaks of women who are sovereign, capable, alive to their own authority.

Her confidence gathers — steadily, naturally.

She understands then that discernment is presence.

Her consciousness has widened. Her attention has returned to herself. And because of that, the world opens within the life she is already living.

With her chosen book resting against her chest, Aurora makes her way toward the front of the shop.

As she passes the final shelves, her eye catches a familiar section nearby.

Shelves of old patriarchal religious texts stand in orderly rows — heavy volumes shaped by authority, hierarchy, and control. She knows them well. She knows their language, their prescriptions, the way they speak about power and obedience, about women and submission. She has lived inside their meanings before.

She recognizes how they once guided her — how they dimmed her light, narrowed her joy, taught her to mistrust her own knowing. Not abruptly, but gradually, through repetition and reverence, through the quiet erosion of self. Yes, and they stole away her women's ways of knowing.

She understands something she could not see before.

These texts are not designed to support her wholeness. They function through control rather than relationship, submission rather than participation. What once passed as spiritual guidance now reveals itself as a system that asked her to disappear in order to belong.

The realization passes through her quickly.

It carries no weight.

What stands out instead is how little resonance remains. The words feel distant, out of step with the living world around her, unable to meet her where she is now.

She does not linger.

Her attention moves easily onward. Her body responds with confidence immediately. Her breath deepens. The room brightens again.

She understands that discernment is not something she applies.

It is something she inhabits.

And from that place, everything she touches begins to reveal itself more fully.

She is ready for what comes next.

And that is enough.

Carrying What Calls Her Forward

Aurora gathers the books she has chosen and carries them to the counter.

The weight in her arms feels satisfying, intentional. Each book rests there because it spoke to her — not urgently, not loudly, but clearly. She places them on the counter one by one, exchanging a few familiar words with the clerk as the total is rung up. There is ease in the interaction, a shared recognition that requires no explanation.

She pays without hesitation.

As she tucks the receipt into her bag, she feels a quiet certainty settle in her body. These books will accompany her forward. They will meet her where she is now — curious, present, ready.

She steps back into the shop's gentle hush one last time, pausing only long enough to take it in. The shelves. The light. The calm intelligence of the space. It all feels complete, held, generous.

When she opens the door and steps outside, the day receives her easily.

The street feels familiar and newly alive at the same time. Her bag rests comfortably at her side. Her steps are sure. There is a subtle lift in her chest — anticipation, interest, a genuine eagerness to begin reading, to enter the worlds waiting for her attention.

She is aware of her future in a new way now.

Not as something distant or undefined, but as something actively unfolding — shaped by her choices, her curiosity, her readiness to engage with what strengthens her. The path ahead feels inviting, rich with possibility.

Aurora walks on with confidence.

She knows where she is going next — home, to read — and she trusts that what follows will continue to meet her at the level of her attention.

She carries her books, her clarity, and her quiet excitement with her.

And she moves forward willingly into what is becoming.

SIX

The End of Potential

Why She No Longer Bonds With What Might Be

She answers the phone. The voice comes to her softly.

It does not rush. It does not insist. It speaks in a way that feels almost familiar — warm, attentive, unhurried. The words are chosen carefully, spaced just far enough apart to leave room for imagination. Nothing is promised outright, yet everything sounds possible.

It invites her to stay.

To wait.

To see what might unfold.

There is a smoothness to it — a practiced ease that feels intimate without being specific. The tone suggests connection, understanding, depth, while never quite arriving anywhere. It leaves space for her to fill in what is missing, to lean forward into what is implied.

For a moment, it works.

She feels the faint pull of it — the old habit of listening closely, of searching for meaning between the words, of mistaking suggestion for presence. The familiar rhythm of *almost* — hums just beneath the surface.

And then something in her shifts.

Not sharply. Not dramatically. Simply and completely.

Her body withdraws its consent.

The sensation is immediate and unmistakable — a quiet closing, a clear internal — NO —that arrives before thought or explanation. What once felt inviting now feels hollow. The warmth dissolves. The spell breaks.

She does not argue with it.

She does not analyze.

She does not stay to understand.

Instead, she smiles — a smile only for herself — and says calmly,

"This isn't working for me. I'm no longer willing to

carry inconsistency. I'm stepping back now. Take care." And then she ends the call.

Aurora does not replay the conversation. There is no echo, no second-guessing, no urge to translate what was said into something kinder or more hopeful than it was. The space left behind is not emptiness. It is composure.

And then she starts laughing — a deep, unrestrained laugh that surprises her with its ease. The laugh of familiarity. The laugh of freedom. The laugh of knowing. In that laughter, *no-more* becomes certain. Whatever once held weight has lost its gravity. She no longer takes him seriously — not with bitterness, not with dismissal — simply with clarity.

The quiet that follows feels clean.

She notices how little effort it took.

What once would have required resolve, rehearsal, or emotional recovery now settles immediately. Her body remains open. Her breath steady. Nothing tightens. Nothing chases after what has already passed.

This is how she knows the shift is real.

She understands now that what once bound her was not love, but anticipation. The subtle bonding that forms around what might become — promises implied rather than offered, futures imagined rather than chosen. Potential had once felt romantic, alive with possibility. But it also asked her to remain unfinished, waiting for someone else to arrive.

She no longer lives that way.

Aurora sees men more clearly now — not as symbols, not as mirrors, not as assignments to be completed — but as they are. Present or absent. Available or not. Interested or not. The clarity is neither harsh nor dismissive. It is simply accurate.

Hope no longer confuses her.

She recognizes how easily hope once stepped in — where presence was missing. How she learned to stay engaged through imagination rather than evidence. How waiting was mistaken for devotion. How intensity was confused with intimacy.

That distinction no longer blurs.

Love, she knows now, does not require interpretation. It does not arrive in fragments or suggest itself through inconsistency. It does not ask her to lean forward, to hold space, to stay open to what refuses to meet her.

Love shows up.

The death of *almost* — feels like relief.

With it goes the quiet labor of staying emotionally available to what never fully arrives. The subtle self-abandonment of waiting. The ongoing hope that effort might turn uncertainty into commitment.

That chapter has closed.

Aurora feels her energy return to her — not dramatically, not all at once, but steadily. Available now for her own life. Her curiosity. Her creativity. Her rest. Her joy. The space once occupied by projection fills naturally with presence.

She does not replace one attachment with another.

She simply stands where she is.

From this place, bonding feels different. Slower. Cleaner. Mutual. She notices how little she initiates now, how naturally she responds instead. How ease has replaced vigilance. How reciprocity has become the quiet requirement she no longer negotiates.

This is not restraint.

It is self-respect lived in real time.

Aurora trusts what meets her. She releases what does not. There is no bitterness in this — only discernment carried forward, embodied and intact.

She understands now that potential is not a promise.

Presence is.

And that understanding shapes everything that comes next.

What She Continues

Aurora returns to the letter she was writing to a friend.

She had left it open when the phone rang.

The page is still there, the pen resting beside it. She picks it up, feeling the small, familiar weight of it settle back into her hand. She rereads the last line she wrote before the phone interruption and lets out a quiet, knowing breath.

She had been writing about waiting.

She notices she no longer does it.

How she no longer stays suspended in conversations that don't arrive, or futures that ask her to imagine herself smaller while she waits to be chosen.

The phone had rung right there.

She notices the coincidence now, clear and unforced, and then continues writing.

She tells her friend that something has shifted. That she feels steadier these days. Less willing to lean forward into uncertainty, less inclined to translate absence into meaning. She writes that she is learning to trust what is present instead of hoping something becomes real.

The words come easily. They don't feel newly discovered — only confirmed.

She does not mention the call.

It doesn't belong in the letter. The page already holds the truth of it. The interruption simply reflected what she was already understanding.

When she finishes, she signs her name and sets the letter aside.

There is a sense of completion in the gesture — not just of the letter, but of something larger. A quiet closing, without ceremony.

Aurora notices how natural it feels to continue.

She gathers herself and moves on with her day, carrying only what is already true.

SEVEN

The Clean Line

Boundaries That Do Not Require Defense

It happens at Seattle's Pike Place Market, where the city opens itself to the sea.

The air carries salt and movement — gulls crying overhead, the sharp scent of fish and brine, the warmth of fresh sourdough bread rising from open doors. The waterfront stretches nearby, ferries gliding in and out, the sound of water lapping against the piers beneath the steady hum of the city and the slow turning of the Ferris wheel. Somewhere close, the aquarium's glass walls hold quiet depths while outside the crowds surge and flow.

Aurora lingers along the waterfront for a moment, letting the rhythm of it settle into her body.

She orders a mustard hot dog from the outdoor stand nearby — the kind eaten standing up, wrapped in paper, uncomplicated and satisfying. She takes a bite and tastes the sharpness of the mustard, the warmth of it grounding her in the moment. It feels good to eat without hurry, without distraction.

A few steps away, she adds a small cup of honey lavender ice cream from a nearby creamery shop — floral, soft, unexpectedly soothing. She carries it to the overlook and eats slowly, watching the ferries crisscross Elliott Bay. White wakes cut clean lines through the water. Boats come and go with quiet certainty, never colliding, never hesitating, each following its own clear route.

The wind lifts her hair. Gulls cry overhead. The city hums behind her, but here, for a moment, everything feels spacious.

She finishes the last bite and wipes her hands, feeling settled, nourished, present.

That's when she sees it.

A large painted sign mounted above the walkway, weathered but unmistakable. A bold hand points upward, finger extended with quiet certainty.

This way to the Pike Place Farmers Market.

She follows the direction of the hand and turns toward the Pike Place Hillclimb.

The steps rise from the waterfront, worn smooth by decades of feet. She begins to climb, unhurried. With each step, the sound of water softens behind her and new layers of the city drift in — voices, laughter, the hum of movement above.

Her breath stays easy. Her pace unforced.

At the top, the market opens around her.

Color first — flowers spilling from buckets in thick, saturated rows. Peonies and sunflowers. Lavender and eucalyptus. The air shifts, sweetness threading through the salt. People move close together now, baskets brushing, conversations overlapping, life pressing in from every direction.

She passes Rachel, the giant bronze pig worn smooth by countless hands and wishes, coins clinking faintly inside her hollow belly. Everything here feels alive — layered, loud, textured, generous.

Aurora moves through it without losing herself.

She is passing the fishmongers' stall on her way toward a small herbal tea shop farther in.

Voices rise and fall in practiced rhythm. A shout cuts

the air. A fish flashes silver as it's thrown cleanly across the counter, landing in waiting hands to cheers and laughter. The crowd compresses and releases in waves, bodies shifting, attention pulled and redirected.

Someone steps back abruptly to avoid the flying fish and bumps into her. Another person reaches across her path, eager for a better view. The space tightens — loud, animated, chaotic.

Once, this kind of moment would have pulled her off center. She would have shifted instinctively, apologized, adjusted her route without noticing she was doing it.

This time, she pauses.

Not abruptly.

Not defensively.

She lets her body register where she is.

Her feet stay planted. Her shoulders remain relaxed. Her breath stays low and steady. She does not move out of her place, and she does not push forward. She simply occupies the space she is already standing in — fully, calmly.

The moment reorganizes itself.

The person who bumped her murmurs an apology and steps aside. The reaching arm withdraws. The crowd reshapes around her without friction, as if responding to a quiet signal she is no longer sending outward.

Aurora feels it immediately — the absence of strain.

Nothing tightens.

Nothing drains.

Nothing follows her.

She continues on, leaving the laughter and shouts behind her as the noise softens. The air shifts again. Shelves of herbs and jars wait ahead, quiet and intentional.

She smiles — not because something was handled, but because nothing needed to be.

This is what the clean line feels like when it is lived.

Aurora no longer prepares herself before speaking.

There is no internal rehearsal, no bracing, no quiet calculation of how her words might land or how they might be received. What she knows arrives already intact. It does not ask for permission. It does not require framing.

Her boundaries are no longer responses. Boundaries with no explanation.

They are conditions.

She notices this now in small moments — the ordinary exchanges where she once would have softened, clarified, or made room for misunderstanding. When something does not align, her body registers it immediately. The line is drawn without effort, without explanation, without tension.

There is nothing sharp about it.

The clean line does not push. It does not punish. It does not perform strength. It simply marks where she ends and something else begins.

She has learned the difference.

Cruelty carries charge.

Self-respect carries calm.

Where cruelty reacts, self-respect remains steady. Where cruelty demands recognition, self-respect requires nothing at all. The clean line does not argue its existence. It stands because it is true.

Aurora no longer negotiates with confusion.

If something arrives inconsistently, unclearly, or asks her to interpret its meaning, she does not lean forward to meet it. She does not try to stabilize what cannot hold its own shape.

Confusion is no longer something she works through.

It is information.

Consistency has become her quiet authority.

Not intensity.

Not insistence.

Not explanation.

Consistency.

What she allows once, she allows again. What she declines, she does not reopen. There is ease in this steadiness — a relief she hadn't known was possible. Her life grows simpler not because she has narrowed it, but because she no longer entertains what disrupts her clarity.

From this place, intimacy feels different.

What comes closer to her now arrives with substance. Words align with action. Interest carries direction. Presence is steady enough that it does not need to be proved. There is no chase, no decoding, no emotional suspense.

Connection no longer asks her to stay alert.

It invites her to relax.

Aurora sees now that the clean line has not narrowed her world.

It has refined it.

What falls away does so quietly. What remains feels obvious in the body — grounded, responsive, whole. She no longer confuses intensity with truth, or persistence with care.

Sovereignty, she understands, is not something she asserts in moments of conflict.

It is something she maintains in moments of choice.

She does not wait to be understood.

She stands where she is.

And from that place, whatever meets her must arrive whole.

Aurora reaches the small herbal tea shop tucked along the market's edge. The scent of dried leaves and flowers greets her — calming, familiar, restorative. She selects a blend with huckleberry and herbs chosen for grounding, for clarity, for warmth. The choice feels instinctive, uncomplicated.

Nearby, she pauses at a flower stall and lets her hand hover before choosing a bundle of fresh-cut blooms. Their colors are vivid, unapologetic. She likes that. She gathers them without second-guessing.

With the tea tucked safely into her bag and the flowers cradled in her arm, she steps back into the flow of the market. There is no rush. No scanning. No adjustment.

She has what she came for.

Not just the tea.

Not just the flowers.

But the quiet confirmation that she moves through the world now without yielding herself to it.

And that is enough.

EIGHT

When the World Responds

She remembered where it had begun.

Not as a story she replayed, but as a bodily fact.

There had been a night—ordinary, unremarkable—when she lay in her bed with her phone beside her, waiting for something that never arrived. A message. A call. Some small proof that her patience would be rewarded this time. The screen dimmed on its own, and the room felt hushed. What she was left with instead was the familiar dense weight of disappointment, settling low in her chest the way it always had.

But that night, something in her reached its limit.

It was exhaustion—clean and final.

She saw, all at once, the life she wanted to leave

behind. The way she no longer wished to live inside her own body. And without bargaining, without another round of explaining it away, something in her simply said, I'm not doing this anymore.

That was the moment her tolerance for nonsense changed.

What followed did not announce itself as transformation. There were no immediate rewards, no sudden clarity from the outside. But inside her body, something had already reorganized. She began to notice how things felt—before she explained them, before she justified them, before she talked herself out of what she knew. There was no more second-guessing herself.

If something tightened her chest or shortened her breath, she paused.

If something left her heavy or hollow, she stepped back.

If something brought warmth or ease, she stayed.

She measured truth by the steadiness in her own system.

And slowly—almost imperceptibly—the world began to respond.

How She Chooses Now

She began to make decisions without rehearsing them first.

For so long, choice had arrived tangled in justification—what she should say, how it would be received, whether it would make sense to someone else. Now, choice surfaced quietly, already complete, before her mind had time to negotiate it away. Her heart was still, at peace.

Her body told her what was true.

Some things carried weight the moment they entered her awareness. A subtle draining that asked more than it gave. When she noticed that feeling now, she let it stand as information.

Other things felt simple. Clear. Neutral in the best way—no spike of hope, no flicker of dread. Just an ease that didn't require vigilance. These were the moments she trusted most. They didn't promise anything extraordinary. They simply held her where she was.

She learned that calm could be trusted.

That steadiness carried its own intelligence.

That desire moved at its own pace.

She learned to move forward with confidence in herself and her choices.

It was safety.

Safety was quietly directive. It showed her where

to linger and where to stop without forcing a narrative around it. It asked her to stay present instead of scanning ahead for reassurance.

When something no longer made sense—when words and actions failed to meet—she settled back into herself. Confusion became a signal she respected.

Trust, for her, meant listening sooner.

She trusted the pause.

She trusted the tightening that said not this.

She trusted the quiet yes that didn't need to be defended.

With that trust came relief. She felt less responsible for carrying conversations, sustaining momentum, or translating herself into forms that might be easier for others to accept. She spoke when it felt true. She declined when it didn't. Silence took its own clear shape.

What mattered held.

What didn't, released.

Something stabilized.

Her days grew simpler—not smaller, but cleaner. She spent less time recovering from interactions that unsettled her. Less time replaying exchanges, wondering what she should have said. Her shoulders softened finally.

Her energy returned to her in small increments, until she recognized it as her own again.

This was the absence of self-abandonment.

And from this place—steady, grounded, unremarkable—she moved through her life trusting what she felt.

How Relationships Reorganize

The changes in her relationships did not arrive as decisions.

They arrived as relief.

Without intending to, she stopped compensating. She no longer filled the spaces where others went quiet. She no longer bridged gaps that weren't hers to cross. When conversations lost their center, she let them drift. When effort became uneven, she noticed—and allowed it to be what it was.

What surprised her was how little resistance there was.

Some people receded almost immediately, as if they had been waiting for her to stop holding the shape of the connection alone. Calls became infrequent. Messages thinned out. Familiar patterns failed to restart. No explanations were offered, and none were required. Distance revealed itself quietly as information.

Other relationships softened rather than disappeared. The urgency fell away, replaced by something quieter. Conversations grew shorter but more honest. Expectations loosened. There was room to breathe without negotiating the space.

And then there were the unexpected ones—the connections that deepened without effort.

With these people, she felt no need to prepare herself. There was an ease in their presence, a sense of being met without performance. They listened when she spoke. They paused when she did. They met her pace.

Her body stayed with her in these moments.

No tightening.

No vigilance.

Just presence.

For the first time, she allowed this to be the measure.

She didn't announce new standards. She didn't explain what she would or wouldn't accept. She stayed present with what felt true. The rest reorganized accordingly.

What once would have registered as loss now clarified

her landscape. She saw that many connections had been sustained by endurance rather than reciprocity.

She recognized love by its gentler tone—by the ease of mutual respect, without the need for justification.

There was steadiness in her relationships now, a reliability she could feel. She arrived as she was, and was received without correction. When there was misunderstanding, it passed. When there was distance, it did not unsettle her.

She trusted herself enough to let relationships show her what they were.

And in doing so, she found herself surrounded—not by more people, but by the right ones.

Life, As It Is Now

Nothing in her life looked extraordinary from the outside.

Her days were made of the same elements they always had—mornings, errands, conversations, small decisions that barely registered as choices. But the way she moved through them had changed. She lived inside the moments as they came.

Some mornings, she noticed the light before anything

else—how it entered the room without asking, touching the edges of things, steady and unremarkable. She moved through those mornings without hurry, letting the day come to her.

She checked in with herself now without ceremony. Not searching for answers, just sensing. A quiet internal calibration that guided her with ease. When something felt right, she stayed with it. When it didn't, she stepped away.

There was no longer a voice in her asking if she was allowed.

She trusted the steadiness in her body more than the promise of anything unproven. She chose what made sense to her, even when it was simple, even when it went unnoticed.

Waiting took on a different shape.

It felt like presence.

Her life grew quieter—not smaller, but more precise. She spent less time recovering from disappointment. Less time reassembling herself after interactions that once took more than they gave. Her energy stayed with her.

And because of that, she was available—to what mattered.

She responded rather than anticipated. She listened without preparing her reply. She allowed moments to complete themselves. There was a dignity in this slowness, a confidence that didn't announce itself—an elegance in her life's cadence.

The world met her differently now. She could feel the difference in the way she breathed. In the way she slept deeply. In the way her body rested into itself.

She lived at the pace of what was already present.

Life continued—ordinary, unremarkable, intact. And within it, she remained steady, listening, moving at the pace her body recognized as true.

There was nothing she needed to return to.
Nothing she needed to anticipate.
This was the life she had seen for herself.
And she was already in it.

The Quiet Between

There was a period she didn't name.

It unfolded without announcement, a space where life continued at a gentler pace. She found herself moving through her days with attention rather than effort, listening more closely to what arose within her.

She moved through her days by listening inward. When something felt aligned, she followed it. When it didn't, she waited. Her intuition became the measure, steady and reliable, shaping each moment as it came. She trusted her own logic and reasoning to support what she already knew.

She no longer felt the need to fill silence with words. Presence did not require commentary. She could remain steady in any circumstance, allowing the right moment to reveal itself before she moved.

During this time, silence felt complete, like a well-formed sonnet. Words arrived only when they belonged. She noticed the way her body settled when she stopped explaining herself, how her breath found its rhythm without instruction.

Her attention turned toward ordinary moments. The weight of her body in a chair. The ease of an unhurried afternoon. The simple satisfaction of letting a moment finish on its own.

Life continued, in tune with what her soul wanted and what felt true.

And within that alignment, something integrated.

In this space, she gave herself permission to be true

to herself—without waiting for reassurance, without needing ideal conditions. She understood that alignment did not promise ease, only clarity. What mattered was not the absence of challenge, but her ability to meet it without abandoning herself.

What she had seen remained present. What she had felt found its place inside her. There was no pressure around it, no urgency to act or define. It lived as knowing—steady, available.

She understood that this space mattered.

Here, readiness formed through consistency. Clarity gathered through presence. Trust grew by listening and responding, again and again.

She stayed there long enough to feel rooted.

And when movement came again, it rose naturally from that steadiness—clear, grounded, already whole.

The world, attentive to this shift, began to respond.

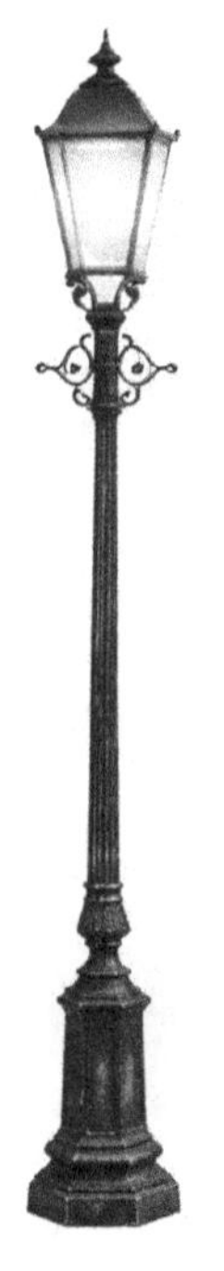

PART IV

The Dawn

NINE

Aurora Rising

Living From Her Center

She no longer searched for herself inside the moment.

She arrived already centered.

There had been a time when she entered situations slightly displaced—attuned to response, prepared for adjustment, alert to what might be required of her. Now, she moved differently. She felt herself anchored from within, steady before anything asked to engage her.

Her body had become an axis.

She noticed this most clearly in moments that once would have unsettled her. A pause in conversation. An unexpected request. A shift in tone. Where she might once have leaned forward, she stayed where she was. Where she might have reached to restore balance, she let balance hold itself.

She did not brace.

She did not disappear.

She remained.

This was sovereignty—not as a stance, but as a state.

The Axis

Her sense of self no longer traveled outward in search of confirmation. It rested in her body, informed by experience, shaped by discernment she trusted.

She did not need to be right.

She did not need to be chosen.

She did not need to be understood immediately.

She noticed how little effort it took now to stay with herself.

Even when something challenged her, it did not unseat her. Discomfort arrived as information, not threat. Difference did not register as danger. She could hold complexity without losing orientation.

Her center stayed with her.

From this place, she spoke when it mattered. She listened without folding herself around what she heard. She moved when movement felt true, and paused when it didn't.

The world no longer determined her posture.

Desire Without Self-Erasure

Desire returned without urgency.

She wanted things now without bargaining for them. Without abandoning herself to pursue them. Wanting no longer felt like leaning forward into uncertainty; it felt like recognition.

She noticed the difference immediately.

Desire did not pull her out of herself. It did not ask her to shrink her needs or soften her boundaries to remain connected. It lived inside her body as clarity rather than hunger.

She could want without losing her footing.

When something aligned, she allowed herself to feel it fully. When it didn't, she did not force the longing to mean more than it did. Desire became an invitation, not a demand.

She did not chase what required her to disappear.

She trusted herself to remain intact—even while wanting.

Love Without Chaos

Love, too, changed shape.

It no longer arrived as intensity that asked her to manage its volatility. It did not require vigilance, interpretation, or endurance. Love felt recognizable now—steady, mutual, grounded in presence rather than projection.

She noticed how her body responded.

With love, she felt more like herself, not less. Her breath stayed even. Her thoughts stayed clear. She did not lose her rhythm trying to match someone else's.

Connection no longer asked her to perform.

She allowed relationships to meet her where she was. When they could, they deepened naturally. When they couldn't, she did not chase their potential.

Love without chaos was not dull.

It was spacious.

It had room to grow.

And within that space, she remained sovereign.

Living Awake

Life continued to present itself as it always had—full of decisions, encounters, uncertainties, and moments that required response. But she met it differently now.

She responded rather than reacted.

She chose rather than endured.

She stayed rather than scattered.

When challenges arose, she did not ask what they meant about her worth. She asked what they required of her presence. When change appeared, she did not rush to control it. She stayed centered and allowed clarity to emerge.

She lived awake.

Not vigilant.

Not guarded.

Awake.

Her days were not perfect. They were real.

She understood now that this was not a place she lived in permanently, but one she could return to—again and again—whenever life pulled at her edges.

And she met them from within herself, grounded in what she knew, available to what mattered.

She did not mistake sovereignty for isolation. She

welcomed connection without surrendering her center. She moved forward without leaving herself behind.

This was not an ending.

It was orientation.

Aurora did not rise as a promise of ease.

It rose as light—revealing what was already there.

And she stepped into her life from the center of herself, awake, present, and sovereign.

EPILOGUE

The Light She Keeps

Life continued to meet her.

Moments arrived that asked for her attention, her care, her presence. Some were ordinary. Some carried weight. She met them as she was, allowing herself to feel what moved through her without losing her center. What endured was her relationship to herself.

When something pressed in, she stayed present. When something pulled, she listened. When a choice appeared, she felt for what aligned and moved from there. Her responses were no longer shaped by urgency, but by recognition.

The light she once noticed at the edges of her life now lived within her days. It was not something she reached for or protected. It was simply how she saw, how she chose, how she remained.

She understood that this way of being did not remove difficulty or guarantee ease. It offered something more durable: orientation. A steady place to return to, again and again, as life unfolded.

Aurora did not rise once and disappear.

It continued—as presence, as perception, as lived experience.

She lived in her own light.

Remember — you are the prize.

ABOUT THE AUTHOR

Glamourgan is a writer, scholar, and philosopher of feminine consciousness whose work explores the quiet architecture of inner transformation, emotional sovereignty, and the moment a woman returns to herself.

She holds a Ph.D. in Metaphysical Sciences, with academic focus on liminality, mythic psychology, and the sacred feminine, and is the author of both scholarly and creative works devoted to women's spiritual and psychological becoming. Her research and teaching have centered on threshold states of identity, embodied wisdom, and the symbolic landscapes through which women reclaim authority over their own lives.

Beyond academia, she has spent many years as a professional intuitive counselor and guide, accompanying thousands of women through periods of awakening, relationship dissolution, self-reclamation, and deep personal reorientation. This lived listening—across cultures, histories, and private moments of reckoning—forms the emotional and psychological ground of her fiction.

The Book of Aurora emerges from this convergence of scholarship and lived human experience. It is not a theory of awakening, but a portrait of it: the quiet, precise moment when endurance gives way to clarity, and a woman steps back into the center of her own life.

Glamourgan lives and writes in the Pacific Northwest, where sea, mist, and long thresholds of light continue to inform her work.

CONTINUE THE JOURNEY WITH GLAMOURGAN

Glamourgan, Ph.D., is the founder of House of Glamourgan, a creative and educational publishing studio devoted to women's wisdom, spiritual sovereignty, and transformative scholarship. Her work bridges myth, psychology, history, and lived spiritual practice, inviting readers into deeper relationship with their own voice, power, and becoming.

In addition to her books, she offers a range of evolving work that may include educational programs, spiritual mentorship, retreats, sacred-site journeys, and curated experiences for women seeking depth, clarity, and renewal.

Readers who wish to explore further titles, upcoming projects, or current offerings are warmly invited to visit:

www.glamourgan.uk

www.houseofglamourgan.com

For speaking engagements, educational collaborations, or event invitations, professional inquiries may be made through the website.

www.ingramcontent.com/pod-product-compliance
Lightning Source LLC
LaVergne TN
LVHW011030110826
845149LV00015B/3366